Once upon a time, there lived a girl named Little Red Riding Hood. She was called that because she wore a hooded red cape every day.

Little Red Riding Hood lived in a beautiful forest, where she enjoyed long walks. She loved everything about the forest: the flowers, the trees, and all the little animals who lived there.

One day, Little Red Riding Hood's mother handed her a basket and said, "I need you to go to your grandmother's house. She is feeling ill. These treats will make her feel better. Now remember— don't stop along the way and don't talk to strangers."

"I won't," Little Red Riding Hood promised, and went on her way.

Little Red Riding Hood was skipping through the forest when a wolf jumped out from behind a tree. "Where are you going, little girl?" asked the wolf.

"Surely Mother didn't mean not to speak to a friendly wolf," thought Little Red Riding Hood. "He seems as nice as any of the other animals in the forest."

"I'm on my way to Grandmother's house. She's not feeling well, so I'm bringing her this basket of goodies to make her feel better," Little Red Riding Hood replied.

"That's nice of you. Does your grandmother live far?" the crafty wolf asked.

"She lives on the other side of the woods. It's not far from here," said Little Red Riding Hood.

As soon as Little Red Riding Hood was out of sight, the wolf ran ahead through the forest to Grandmother's house. He snuck inside and hid the sick woman in the closet.

To disguise himself as Grandmother, the wolf put on her nightcap and gown. Then, he tucked himself into her bed and waited for Little Red Riding Hood to arrive.

When Little Red Riding Hood knocked at Grandmother's door, a gruff voice called out, "Who's there?"

"It's me, Little Red Riding Hood, with goodies for you, Grandmother," she replied.

"Open the latch and come in, dear," replied the wolf, trying to sound like Grandmother. When Little Red Riding Hood opened the door, she stared at her poor, sick grandmother.

Little Red Riding Hood was certain
her Grandmother must be very ill,
for she looked very strange indeed.
"Why Grandmother," she said,
"What big ears you have!"

"The better to hear you with,
my dear," answered the sneaky wolf.

"Grandmother, what big eyes
you have!" she exclaimed.

"The better to see you with,
my dear," said the wolf.

Little Red Riding Hood feared something was terribly wrong. "Grandmother, what big teeth you have!" she said, as she moved back toward the door.

"The better to EAT you with, my dear!" shouted the wolf as he leapt from the bed towards Little Red Riding Hood.

"Help! Help!" shouted Little Red Riding Hood, running from the house.

A huntsman saw the wolf chasing the little girl. When the wolf ran by, the huntsman hit the wolf over the head with the butt of his rifle.

"Run and see if your grandmother is all right. I'm going to take this nasty wolf into the woods. You'll never see him again," said the huntsman to Little Red Riding Hood.

"Grandmother! Grandmother!" called Little, Red Riding Hood. Then, she heard a muffled sound coming from the closet and there Little, Red Riding Hood was happy to find her grandmother safe and sound.

When the huntsman returned, Grandmother opened the basket of goodies. The three of them ate a delicious lunch and Grandmother felt much better.

THE END